PARTNERS
in
RHYME

LIFE WRITTEN IN POEM VERSE

PARTNERS
in
RHYME

J'AIME ÉCRIRE
LYRICAL the POETESS

*This is a book about
life written in poem verse
to inspire and touch the
hearts of its readers.*

Thank you for indulging us.

J'AIME ÉCRIRE

Dedication

This book is dedicated to the loves of my life, my children: DéVaughn-Anthony Griffith, Lance Warren Knuckles, Jazmyne Mae Knuckles, and Julius Earl Cole. You all are the world to me.

To future kings, my grandsons:
Jaylyn-DéVaughn Griffith, Deon-Anthony Griffith, Julius Jamir Cole, and Boston King Cole

and

To future queens, my granddaughters:
Lailah Renee Cole, Skye Amara Cole and Madison Echerverria, I love you to the moon and back.

To Tabia Hunt, thank you for loving my son.

A special dedication goes to my baby sister, Lyrical the Poetess who has been there for me through everything.

To my sister, Naomi Hunter and my brother, James O. Hunter, I love you so much.

To my brother-in-law, Bradley Knuckles, thanks for everything.

To Julius Knuckles, again, thank you.

To my Aunt Barbara H. Paige, Aunt Julia Best and Aunt Diane Tillman, I love you all.

To my stepmother, Mary B. Hunter, I love you.

To my parents: James M. Hunter and Gladys A. Tillman; my grand-mothers: Ethel M. Tillman-Foster and Callie M. Hunter (the woman who raised me to be the woman that I am today); my aunts: Dorothy H. Hinton and Myra M. Satterfield; my uncles: Ernest J. Tillman, Raymond E. Tillman, George B. Tillman, Eddie Best, and Theartis Hinton, may you all rest in peace.

Acknowledgments

Special thanks to Joan Vassar, for her many contributions and Tamara Wells-Braxton, for her support and encouragement.
I also want to give accolades to Antonio Cannon (King Purple) who enticed my writing, to Mac Tsunami who stimulated my writing, to Eric "EBear" White who inspired me to write, to Mike Sudler who motivated me to write and to the entire 72-Hour Weekend Freestyle Writers crew who encouraged me to write.

Special honors go to Mark Lawless, Troy Ulysses Davis, Judith Hicks, Aquila Coulibaly, Robin Janette Pauley, Janae Stewart, Ron Frankbless Murphy, Anthony Ligon and Sherry Kimwana Ligon. Thank you all.

To my FKC team, thank you for everything.

LYRICAL THE POETESS

Dedication

I would like to dedicate this book to my husband, Mr. Christopher Terrance Mote for his loving support in all of my endeavors. Thank you so much.

I also dedicate this book to the reasons why I breathe, fight, and live... my beautiful daughters, starting with my firstborn, Ms. Davina Darlene Washington, and my baby, Mrs. Monique Marie Lawrence.

Let's not forget the rest of my legacy, my first and only granddaughter and princess, Miss Jaidah Jay (Jaidah Arianna Abubey) next, my firstborn grandson and prince, Master Michael Owen Lawrence, my second grandson and prince, Master Kenneth Dwayne Johnson III and last but not least my third grandson and prince, Master Aiden Monroe Lawrence.

A special dedication goes to the Co-author, and my big sister, Ms. J'aime Écrire. This beautiful woman is the matriarch of my family and my inspiration. She told me that I had this gift and to use it to inspire. She also helps me to dream big and live my dreams. "Without your support, this wouldn't be possible. I love you!"

In loving memory of my mother, Gladys Ann Tillman, I love you and miss you dearly.

Acknowledgments

Special acknowledgment goes out to some of my family and friends who supported and inspired me along the way. Thank you to the 72-Hour Weekend Freestyle Writers crew and organizer, Mr. Antonio Cannon.

Special thanks to those who supported, loved, and encouraged me to continue this journey:
Lance Knuckles, Naomi Hunter, Kamisha McCullough, Deborah Cowan, Stephanie Perry, Judith Hicks, Aquila Coulibaly, Robin Janette Pauley, Janae Stewart, Evergreen Washington, Delane McCloud, James Oliver Hunter, Eric "EBear" White, Anthony Ligon, Sherry Kimwana Ligon, Troy Ulysses Davis, Mark Lawless and Ron Frankbless Murphy.

TABLE OF CONTENTS

J'aime Écrire

TABLE OF CONTENTS

Lyrical the Poetess

J'aime Écrire

J'aime Écrire

I WISH I WERE A POET
J'aime Écrire

I wish I were a Poet.

If I were a poet, I would write poems
so profound, so sublime,
with mad rhythm and even madder rhyme.

I would be classified as a poetess
and my words would be more famous than myself.

Each spoken syllable would paint a picture,
provide visual sustenance, and nourish the mind.

Wisdom flowing, intellect towing, cerebral stimulation-
Binary off and on switches, circuits-prolific...

Oh, how I wish I were a poet.

I wish I were a Poet.

If I were a poet, I would recite literary knowledge
like that of Shakespeare and RUN-DMC.

Innuendos, metaphors,
figures of speeches, and analogies.

"To be or not to be"; "In the beginning";
"It was the best of times, it was the worst of times"

and "Two years ago, a friend of mine,
asked me to say some MC rhymes."

Oh, how I wish I were a poet.

Poetical, poetically.
It's how you say what you say
that makes it poetry.

Anyone can make words rhyme
but it's the light that goes on
that makes the words shine.

Imparting knowledge,
Intellectual degrees are the reward
for the life that words breathe.

"In the beginning was the Word,
and the Word was with God,
and the Word was God."

Before your words can breathe life,
you need God's Word, the Word… Word!

"I think therefore I am."

Oh, how I wish I were a poet.

CONCEPTION
J'aime Écrire

Missed periods, nausea, morning sickness, aches, pains, and unusual appetites. What could be wrong?
I don't know, but something, something just ain't right.

Up until now, I thought my life was complete but something is growing inside of me and I can't sleep.

Tossing and turning, inexplicable dreams, mixed emotions, and maybe I shouldn't have eaten those collard greens...
before going to bed.

I feel weaker, yet stronger.
A metamorphosis is going on right within my own being.
Revitalization. Life. A spirit of growth and aspirations.

Artificial Conceptions
Regurgitating all negativity and failures of my past.
Using them as lessons instead of burdens.
I can't keep anything down. I feel like I'm about to explode.

I can't breathe!

This life inside of me is getting stronger,
kicking harder to be released.

Second Trimester
Oh my God! I can hardly contain myself.
How do I enter this new journey, epidural or natural?
God or man, to whom do I owe my allegiance?
Where did these passions come from?
I guess I was born with them.

Ectopic:
In life, some things have to die for other things to be born.

Premature:
I need spiritual guidance to direct my path.

Multiple Births:
There are just so many gifts God has instilled in me.

Nursery:
How will I address it?
What color will my visions be painted?
How will I nurse this, bottle-fed or abreast?
There are so many things that must be done.
I'll have to change my diet and pass some tests.

Delivery:
No longer a child but a woman full-grown
Maybe I'll have a coming-out party…
No, not like that!

I mean, coming out of my shell and coming into my own.
There are so many options to consider.
Failure, I can't afford.

I need to be healthy: mind, body, and spirit,
after all, I have a dream to support!

INCOMPLETION
J'aime Écrire

I've never been one to finish what I started
Excusing myself with excuses

Resulted in incomplete dreams being unfulfilled
Legitimate reasons for unsuccess

Genius mentality arrested in mess, created by me
Not allowing the creator to create in me

That which was meant for me,
revealing my ultimate destiny

What's this all about, what does it mean?
Is life not what it seems to be?
Is this really all there is for me?

I stepped up to the challenge, stepped up my game
Challenged myself, redirected my aim

Now I'm shooting for the stars...
that's too close you see
I'm shooting for something much greater, the galaxy

Heaven's in my view, you can't see me
I'm far above average, I'm unique, I'm me

Incompletion, no longer in my vocabulary
College, GPA 4.0, Dean's List,
President's Honor Roll, Computer Science degree

It's only the beginning, there's plenty more to see
To be continued... NOT incomplete

IT'S GONNA BE GOOD TOO
J'aime Écrire

I have loads, many, I mean lots of unfinished poems
Just stores of my thoughts and inspirations

Waiting for me to get to that point in my life
where I've reached my aspirations

I'm like an unfinished story waiting to be written
asking for God's direction as I proceed

I guess the reason that my work is in process
is because I'm a work in process indeed

I haven't given up on the process
It's just the process is processing
what's been processed while yet processing

I have many years of experience
(that's slang for what I've been through)

I'm not exactly sure when I'll be finished,
but when I do,
it's gonna be good too

BORN-AGAIN LOVE
J'aime Écrire

Being in love is a wonderful feeling, a bit euphoric even. It's been quite a while since I've experienced this sense of ecstasy but I am open to the opportunity. I'm just a bit more conscious about depicting what is fiction versus what is reality.

I don't regret my past experiences for they have molded me into who I am. I am just glad that I am who I always was and who I will always be but more mature and wiser, the more experienced me.

I feel a sense of love in the air, and to some in my position that would scare. I'm not afraid to tread the grounds that others wouldn't dare.

My imagination has gotten away with me. It has me thinking about our future and all of the wonderful possibilities.

Even if what I've imagined doesn't manifest a return, I'm excited about our friendship and the yielded rewards that we will earn.

There's nothing better than true friendship which is where a love affair should begin. No matter how this relationship develops, friends, we'll be to the end.

It feels like love at first sight, although, I've been looking for a while. The thought of your intimate touch often makes me smile. I'm feeling like a kid again, you bring out my inner child.

The love in me has been born again, and I owe it all to you, my friend.

A GEM
J'aime Écrire

The most precious gems are known to be found
within the uttermost depths of soil in the ground.
So perfectly flawed, a rare find of like minds and kindred spirits.

Your significance is priceless which can't be measured in
currency and currently, I appraise you with the highest esteem.
My greatest desire is to adorn myself with the essence of your
being.

Freeing my soul of the debris of counterfeit sticks and stones
which injured my emotions and left me feeling isolated and
alone. Everything that glitters isn't gold.

I welcome the radiance that comes from your internal source
which has externally given me a glow that only love can emit
from the true light force.

You are the greatest compliment to my complement and
supplementary, I trust you.

When two souls are meant to be together, there is a
magnetic force of attraction that can't be explained, and by
many comprehended.

There's a circular radius that has no beginning or ending and
must be calculated in diameters. The pi of you and I.

Mutual respect and admiration are only the beginning and the
continuance has no ending. You complete me.

ECSTASY
J'aime Écrire

With only the sound of the beats of our hearts
as we lay in the quiet of the night

I feel safe and secure in your arms
when you kiss and hold me so tight

Having you next to me is ecstasy

Sharing intimacies that we wouldn't normally share
Breaking the silence, whispers without a care

I'm here for you, hoping you'll always be there
You have me feeling like love is in the air

The two of us sharing
moments of laughter and kid-like play
There are so many things that my spirit wants to say

Words are not necessary
You're reading my innermost thoughts

Having you relate to me is ecstasy

I believe you are who you say you are
but actions speak louder than words

Not Show-n-Tell, but Show-n-Prove
The pudding is the proof

When we see each other,
it's always eye-to-eye

Physically, Emotionally and Spiritually
Being in your presence is the ultimate ecstasy

I LOVE YOU, I DO
J'aime Écrire

As we venture on this eternal journey together
I can't imagine life without you
I love you, I do

What are the odds that there can be heaven on earth?
Instead of pinching myself, I'm going to pinch you
If you feel it, then I will too
We are one spirit composed of two

Each minute apart seems like an eternity
because without you, there's no we

I visualize your face, your smile, your wild boy style
I miss this feeling of rhapsody, it's been a while

Your essence keeps creeping into my dreams
I believe this is heaven or so it seems

I don't want to be awakened unless it's by you
I love you, I do

DO WHAT YOU GOTTA DO
J'aime Écrire

I have to love you for who you are
not the way you look but the way
your spirit speaks to my heart

This is not a portrait, but a work of art
Priceless memories already etched in my mind
of me being yours and you being mine

I couldn't stand anything ever happening to you
so please, my love, do whatever you gotta do

Make sure our future is secure
I'm not an expert, I'm learning as well
I'll help you if you help me too

We've been afraid of failure, as well as success
It's strategy, like in the game of chess
I've been plagued with a few stalemates
now it's time for checkmate with my king and soulmate

You're just enough for me
I've never had enough on my plate

Hungrily, I've starved until
I dissipated and lost faith

I look forward to spending
our wealth of abundant love and health
There's a whole lot more to say,
but I'll wait until we're by ourselves.

I believe in you
so again, my love, do what you gotta do

DESTINY
J'aime Écrire

What happens when you find out your king is not?
And as a jester, you discover the wrought
Bent out of shape, a mistake on your part

How do you fix it and relinquish what you lost?
Time doesn't rewind, so you travel apart
From a distance, it looks hopeless
then you find hope-ness (happiness)
and less stress when two minds beat as one heart

For what seems like an eternity, you've resisted
Never imagined that this type of oneness existed
True inspiration develops from within
when it feels like your life has begun again

Luck, don't believe in it... fate
Divine and purposed intentions at any rate
Synchronicity, seemingly unrelated events
Proving to be more than mere coincidence

No one has the ability to alter this,
not even you and me

What was meant to be shall be
Destiny

GIFTED
J'aime Écrire

I'm gifted, prolific, don't get it twisted
I didn't invent it, but I'm about to perfect it

My vernacular, spectacular
Taking the ordinary to extraordinary,
nothing manufactured

Some people are just extra
The original, the real, is what I'm after

They say the truth hurts
I'm prepared to endure
The equivalent of true love,
unadulterated and pure

Bring something to the table
Show me you're about it, capable, able
Oh, and by the way, I'm gonna need that table

Don't expect more from me
than what you're willing to give
My dictum on life
Live and let live

I'm a grown woman looking for a man of the same
Seduce me, entice me and make love to my brain

Flowers and material gifts are nice too,
but what my heart yearns for is the quintessence of you

MY KING (Where Are You?)
J'aime Écrire

Excuse me, sir, I was wondering, have you seen my king?
I'm not sure, but I think I've been abandoned because all I have
is this ring.

I have some babies; some princes, and princesses who aspire
to the throne. How do I elevate them when their father, their
highness, their king is gone?

I've looked high and low and lo and behold, there's still no sign
or, is this the sign I've been looking for? Are we at war?

Is he fighting for the sake of his family?
Maybe, he's been taken hostage and can't escape from
the enemy.

I've entreated the help of the wise men of counsel,
yet they're dumbfounded without a clue.
I implore thee, my king, where are you?

Don't you love us anymore?
Where is that glimpse of hope?
Have you lost the luster in your crown,
or is it that you're currently at peace
and don't want to be found?

WHO AM I?
J'aime Écrire

Who am I? I often ask myself.
Giving up me to please you
until there's none of me left.

I'm giving up, giving up me for the sake of you.
I'm not giving up;
I'm just giving up for the sake of you.
I'm tired but less confused.

I don't always know exactly what I want,
but I do know exactly what I don't want.
I don't want to feel used or abused.

To each their own and every individual
has their own definition for the terminology used.

I don't want to argue or fight about semantics
or rave and rant about what's important to me.

If it's not important to you,
then I'll let you live in peace.
You don't have to worry about pleasing me.

I'll adjust to those little idiosyncrasies.
I'll worry about pleasing me.

If the sight of the forest
becomes obscured by the trees,
I'll climb out of the thick of it so I can see.
I can see clearly now the pain is gone.

My experiences have taught me a lot,
like when enough is enough
and when I'm done.

RUN AWAY
J'aime Écrire

No matter how positive I attempt to be
I'm surrounded by unmeasurable amounts of negativity

I guess there's some cynicism in even me
I couldn't see the forest for the trees
I once was blind, but now I see

I'm running away today
but before I do, I must pray

Lord, please guide my steps so I don't stray
I'm not sure which way I should sway
but today has been a hell of a day
and I don't think I can take it this way
I'm not sure if I even want to make it this way

If you don't hear from me, don't worry, I'm okay
I just took some time to run away

LORD, YOU KNOW I DIDN'T WANT THIS...
J'aime Écrire

Lord, You are so faithful and true. You've given me the desires
of my heart and abounded my every need.
 In your word, You said, ask, and I shall receive.

I asked and You furnished,
but Lord, You know I didn't want this.

We know not what we ask for, praying and pleading in vain.
Thinking only of ourselves and how to satisfy selfish gain.

I asked and You furnished,
but Lord, You know I didn't want this.

I prayed for a vessel of the male anatomy, not clarifying
the worth and values. You're awesome forevermore and
again, my Lord, I thank you.

I asked and You furnished,
but Lord, You know I didn't want this.

My prayers changing lanes daily while discernment merges
and intertwines. Patience and strength on the side street,
now wisdom, knowledge, and understanding abide.

I asked and You furnished.
With an open heart, I receive and yes,
I accept and I do want this.

BRANDING
J'aime Écrire

Is this rhetoric chatter,
or just another chant louder than the latter?

As a matter of fact, the fact of the matter is
all of the ranting and raving just makes people madder
but the solution has been obliterated in wasteful matter.

What if we come up with a realistic solution
instead of grandstanding?
We can begin with self-branding.

Back in slavery times (no pun intended, cause we're still in it),
branding signified property and depicted who owned it.

We are so disloyal,
nowadays, we voluntarily brand ourselves.
Ironically, not with our own names but everyone else's.

Is it necessary to have the latest name brand?
Does that make us feel like we fit in?
Why exactly would we want to fit in a society meant
to enthrall? Paying for products and services not meant
for us at all.

We perpetuate our own enslavement.
Investing billions of dollars without the return of any cents.
Let us stop and think about how this doesn't make any sense.
We've become an offense instead of our own defense.

Supporting the oppressor with a personal-assist
while they fake-shot us to death.

How can we ever be free
when we're enslaved with slavery mentality?

GENOCIDE
J'aime Écrire

Killing my dreams, starting with my offspring
has me wondering, what the future will bring
or if there is a future in this life thing.

The hurt that I feel for others,
my nation's siblings... sisters and brothers.

This doesn't just happen in faraway places.
It's in my own backyard, amongst the races.

We are a majority but minority in our thinking.
Forced over on a ship that is constantly sinking.

This hatred pains my heart.
Our culture's barely thriving.

Our generation is on life support
and our children are continually dying.

Lord, help us from this evil madness.
Have mercy on us, I'm crying...

RESTITUTION
J'aime Écrire

Enslavement: Poverty. Restitution.
40-acres and a mule?
Replaced with 40 hours and the slave master's rule.

Institution: Mental prison, domino-driven, pollution...
What's the solution?

Ensnared by prayer and random chants of despair
has gotten us nowhere.

Where is the help, the assistance, the relief?
All I've witnessed is pain and grief.
Desperately seeking release
from the hatred and bigoted reprise.
Back on my knees another day
cause all I know how to do is pray.

It helped me get through obstacles so many times before.
God has opened doors when there was no door.
I walked through valleys that were not green,
full of chaos and turmoil, or so it seemed.
Not fully understanding what it all meant.
Trials and tribulations were heaven sent.

It took those challenges to move me to another place.
Changed my thought process, put negativity to rest.

Even when hard-pressed,
I will never again second guess
the power of God and despite any test,
I am too blessed to be stressed.

ACCUSATORY TONE
J'aime Écrire

Calling me all day and night
with your accusatory tone
Asking me where I am,
and when will I be home?

With your vibrating temper
and your annoying persistence
Demanding an answer from me
when I offer resistance

You're not going to control me
I've had enough of that in my life
We just began getting to know each other
I am not your wife

Every day you switch up on me
forever changing your style
Getting all touchy-feely
Behaving mega butt wild

Acting like you're networking
You work when you wanna work

Talking about how it's slow
I'm just counting down the minutes
for you to go

There are plenty of fish in the sea
and a new bait every day

I'm about to school ya
"You gon' learn today"

I'm my own person
and I don't have to listen
to a thing you gotta say

You don't hear me anyhow
What a price to pay

"Can you hear me now?"
If not, that's okay

Roaming all over the place
You never have time for me

Your days are always occupied
and your weekends are never free

I need quality time
and unlimited access
You can't compare apples to oranges

You never miss the well
'til there is no well

Oh well, what the hell
I just got an advertisement in the mail
So long sucka! I'm getting a new cell

CRIMINAL INTENT
J'aime Écrire

I apologize sir but no outsiders allowed
You're going to need to stand with the crowd

A Police officer? Lieutenant?
I'd never guess from the looks of it
You appear as a bystander from your look

You must be undercover
I guess that's why they say,
don't judge a book by its cover
or a cover by its book

All these questions!
Where was I at the time in question?
Well, where do I begin?
I was at a press conference until about ten

Officer, I don't need to lie
I have a perfect alibi

On the way to the meeting
I stopped to get something to eat
I don't remember the name, let me get my receipt

You know, one of them fancy joints
for ballers and big wigs
You get the point

When I left, I broke my heel
so I went to the mall to get some shoes
What else could I do?

Just the facts?
Sir, these are the facts

The shoes were gold and black
with a strap attached
Now, what woman could pass on that?

I don't mean to brag
but it was a perfect match for my designer handbag

It was bad, meaning good
That's what they say in the hood

Was I seen?
But of course, I was seen
I looked too good not to be seen
The dress, by the way, was money green

I was killing 'em
It was homicide, if you know what I mean?
I know, I know... just one more thing

What is it this time?
Exactly, what is the crime?
So, I'm being charged for my killer lines?

Oh, is that it?
Okay, okay, I admit
I must confess...
I DID IT!

RIDE OR DIE
J'aime Écrire

This up and down relationship is making me dizzy
Got my nerves in a frenzy

I tried to enter with caution
but been caught in your snare
Locked in, no escape anywhere
I want to act like I don't care
Truth is, I'm scared

Trying to be brave,
a trooper for the cause
Just waiting to exhale
in case I need to pause

Voluntary victim
It's nobody's fault, but my own
I can handle this
after all, I'm grown

Taking me to huge heights
and dropping me in a flash
Trying to ride but I feel like I'm gonna die

There is just one question I gotta ask
How long is this phenomenon gonna last?

My emotions covered up by tears
The pit feeling in my stomach
reminds me of my fears

Screams, drowning out my screams
Lightning-speed bolster
Lord, help me, please!
Never again, will I ride a roller coaster

FRIEND OR FOE
J'aime Écrire

You are getting on my nerves!
It's time to split, this has got to end
You're more like a foe than a friend

Turning on me like a Boston terrier
No black or white, just areas of gray areas

I need some clarity about our relationship
Should we try to salvage or just sever our ties?
When it seems like we're growing,
it turns out to be lies

Like colored-dye,
you're shady with so many hues
I don't have a clue what to do with you

You're messing up my swag
It's like playing tag, you're it
I'm so tired of dealing with this

I try to wash my hands of you
but you got me conditioned
Can't live with or without you

I declare, in despair
I'm gonna cut you off
and grow some new hair

WEIGHT DESPAIR
J'aime Écrire

This balancing device is very nice,
so sleek and stylish and digitized.
I can't wait to test my size...
"Damn! Damn! Damn!" Those fries!

What the hell? Lies you tell!
And you call yourself a scale?

Where's the justice in all of this?
It's a travesty, an outrage, an atrocity.
I put my trust in you and in return you just mock me?

Well, I'm not giving up this easy.
Oh God! Let me pray.

Lord, please remove all unwanted cellulite that is trying to destroy
my figure. Let me not be tempted to get a second helping.
Teach me patience and portion control.
Allow me to set and attain my goals.

Now, I know what time it is.
It's back to biz, I'm on my grind.
It's time to leave this behind, behind.
Well, maybe, I'll keep that behind of mine.

I'm tired of all of these dieting woes.
So how much do you subtract for clothes?

I'll just take them off. That'll shed some pounds,
or ounces, or grams or some unit of sort.
You know, I appear heavier because I'm short.

The oil, the water, the barrette in my hair,
that's what's causing this weight despair.

The music's too loud, I'm breathing too hard.
Those dang kids playing out in the yard.

Causing me pain and excessive weight gain.
If you think this is the end,
then you got another thing coming.

WRITER, NOT A FIGHTER
J'aime Écrire

I've decided to treat myself better
so that I can treat you better
It's a win-win situation

Feeling this way about you makes me write better
I'm a writer, not a fighter so I fight better
No matter the outcome, I'll come out better

My past relationships have left a bad taste in my mouth
but I am not bitter

It's survival of the fittest
and for that I'm fitter
There's more than meets the eye
I learned that everything that glitters...

You've governed my path, so I walk straighter
and patterned my speech, now I'm an orator

No matter the circumstance
"I'll be back" like the Terminator

You added -er to my great
so now I'm greater

The governor of my life
You're my administrator

All things work for the good
when you have faith and labor

In the beginning, was the Word
and the Word is God

Greater is the You in me than he that's in the world
Emitting my light so the truth unfurls

Having something and losing it
can be worse than not ever having it at all

I'm running with this thing called life
so, I can't drop the ball

Your super on my natural is supernatural
The seed implanted in me has manifested wherewithal

You've elevated my psyche to a greater plane
I'll try to explain it so that it's simple and plain

I trust in you, don't know any other way
I'm tired of worrying, I've learned how to pray

Not only are you my God, but you are my friend
The spirit in me is Alpha and Omega
Amen and Amen again

SAVED
J'aime Écrire

He offered me a bite and I did eat, later learning that this was
a tactic of defeat. The knowledge didn't make me any wiser. It
just made me feel naked and afraid. What a bed I had made.
To lie in it meant death and lack of acknowledgment of self.
And for this, I gave up all of my wealth believing there was
somehow better on the other side. He only got to see two sides
of me, love or hate while missing out on the full spectrum that
truly lies within. The uncompromising lies and affliction of pain
caused my soul to cry out like in the epitaph of Cain.

He thought he had it great because of his full plate, not
realizing the dessert which he was never privy of. There's a lot
of me to be admired and can only be inspired and reciprocated
by true love. What could he have been thinking of? Greed and
self-centeredness caused him to miss the essence of me and
experience the meaning of true bliss. I never knew or wanted
to know love like this.

Coming to the realization that this was by no means
love, I equated it to hate and became venomously irate.
Vindictiveness, revenge, and the settling of scores, but then
I remembered, "Vengeance is mine saith the Lord." After
determining that I couldn't take anymore, I decided to leave
the hatred at the door. No longer mad, I wandered around in
the wilderness until I found what I was meant to see. I heard an
angelic voice speak out to me.

"This is where you were meant to be, me with you and you
with me." The truth of light shined so bright, that I was blinded
by the rays. Baptized by repentance and forgiveness,
I knew that I had been saved.

ON MY KNEES
J'aime Écrire

Forgive me, LORD, for I have sinned.
How do I start over and begin again?

The LORD asked, "Who you rolling with?"
I fell to my knees and began to repent.
There was no mistaking HE was heaven sent.

Hell-bent on doing things my way,
I realized my errs and began to pray.

LORD, give me this day, my daily bread.
I know there are better days ahead.
With this knowledge, I am fed.
The LORD is my shepherd as I am led.

Not sure whether to go left or right,
I can't go wrong if I do what's right.
Increasing the vision of my sight,
out of the darkness, into the light.

Lyrical the Poetess

Lyrical the Poetess

WHO AM I???
Lyrical the Poetess

Who am I???

Love's in the air, a true love affair. Ink married pen when my poetry began. Feelings and emotions spilled onto a blank canvas create pure magic of imagination mixed with creativity. I hope we have longevity and prosper as we touch hearts. Bringing minds of all sorts together with the knowledge we impart.

We unite on an intellectual level as I allow them to gain insight into my world full of wonder. Shared experiences, deep thoughts, and raw truths that make you ponder. My mind is an adventure all the time.

Metaphors, Hyperboles, Puns, and Similes all intertwined.

I never know what thoughts will be penned.
I just let nature take its course as I express what's within.

It's invigorating yet therapeutic.
Relieves stress and uplifts.
I'm addicted to this love affair, this gift.
Revealing parts of who I am so you too can know it.

Who am I???
I'm just a Poet.

A BEAUTIFUL MIND
Lyrical the Poetess

Mixing rhymes with rhythm, verses with flow,
giving you intellectual pleasure for your artistic ego.

Stimulating your psyche on all kinds of levels still taking it up a
notch. This is a gift signed, sealed and delivered, not botched.

Deep thoughts and emotions bubble forth in abundance like
downpours of rain. It's so prolific, it cannot be contained.

The ability to move people with ink and words may seem absurd
until it happens to you and you feel the power of these
verbs in action. It draws you in like a physical attraction.

Satisfaction as I arouse emotions and build on man's intellect with
my dialect that spills forth as my pen moves something within.

Releasing metaphors, relating parables, drawing on hearts.
Sometimes it's subliminal like abstract art.

It's phenomenal yet profound how creative talents unbound
in the binders of my mind. Let's sit back, enjoy and unwind.

Let Lyrical's therapy relax your mind as my wheels
keep spinning lines like fine linen.

Don't fight it. Embrace it.
Let it inspire you. The brain is so complex, yet beautiful.

SUNSHINE
Lyrical the Poetess

Wake up feeling renewed
Sun on my face, imbued

It's a new day, another chance
to embrace life, to enhance

Stay balanced, honest, humbled, and grounded
Encircle like-hearted ones, well rounded

Encompass wisdom, share knowledge to relate
Draw images on their heart to emulate

Rays of beauty left behind
Reflection of my sunshine

GUIDANCE
Lyrical the Poetess

From the beginning of days starting with Adam n Eve.
Independence from God has brought destruction to say the least.

Demons within us bring out the worst.
Born into sin at the start from the day of our birth.

Looking for guidance from man instead of the Most-High
has proven detrimental to our lives,
leaving us blinded, this I can't deny.

Free will is a gift, if used correctly, brings peace.
Misuse of this gift serves Satan and the six-headed beast.

Stop allowing our minds to be twisted and misled.
Search for God and his Son, the living bread.

Allow them to teach us through the word of truth
as this wicked world is passing.

Follow the guidance of the Most High
and live a life that is everlasting.

FREEDOM
Lyrical the Poetess

Freedom
Will I ever be free?

Freedom
Free to be me in a world full of debauchery and hypocrisy

Freedom
Can I really be me?

Freedom
Let it ring. Lift up my voice to sing, to dream

Freedom
To be the best me I can be

Freedom
From racism, strife and foolish pride

Freedom
I just want to be free to live my life

Freedom
Not just for me... for all to be blessed

Freedom
Is what I quest

Freedom
To bring to life, written words
from a page to a stage

Freedom
Is what I crave

Freedom
To touch souls, young and old;
free to be confident and bold

Freedom
Is it a realistic goal?

Freedom
To be at peace in a world full of uncertainties

Freedom
Isn't it what we all need? Don't you agree?

Freedom
What does it mean to be truly free?

Freedom
If I let you be you, and you let me be me

Freedom...

SUBLIMINAL
Lyrical the Poetess

Subliminal messages are not seen as clear as day.
Motions and notions move something in you with nothing
to say.

Body language speaks louder than words can convey.
Completely undress your conscious to view and display.

Impressions mixed with wrong expectations from the start.
Images in your mind don't always align with someone else's
heart.

With messages unspoken yet redefined like abstract art.
Look beyond the physical as your emotions begin to impart.

Intentions of the heart, your brain never knew existed.
Unconsciously allow your mind to conform.
You just can't resist it.

This stimulus or mental process got your psyche twisted.
It's subliminal because the message was clear
but you missed it.

THE ???
Lyrical the Poetess

Situation is bleak. Full of pain, lies, abuse, and deceit.
When first love takes a back seat, knees no longer get weak.

I hate to hear the words you speak, can't even
have a decent convo. Do I stay or Do I go?

Pictures hold beautiful memories of what used to be; however,
as time goes on images change and gets distorted.
The need to please one another, aborted.

Love becomes like faded memoirs; gloves are off.
No more masks.
Can a love like this last?

Feeling restrained yet bound by a love full of strings,
staying intertwined. Hmm... How will this love be defined?

Will it last a lifetime and make history or will it be
defeated by quarrels, emotions, and idiosyncrasies?

It's crazy that I have to even contemplate
the thought of leaving though.
Do I Stay or Do I Go?

That is the question.

HIDDEN SCARS
Lyrical the Poetess

I often wonder can they tell, please don't let them see me.
I'm too ashamed to be exposed so
I keep myself covered under all these clothes.
No one needs to know who I am. Who would care anyway?
That's what the painter who paints me always says.

At first, when people glance at me,
they shockingly gasp,
"Oh my God, what happened to you?"
My canvas feels their sympathy.
It's definitely a sight for sore eyes underneath the pain and the lies.
Then I turn colors and fade away.

In that brief moment, my canvas feels safe and renewed
until the painter stains it again with domestic abuse.
The canvas tries to keep me a secret from the rest of the world.
It has more fear of what people think, than the painter and his ink.

I'm a constant reminder of the love the painter has for her.
Just look at me, I'm all black and blue.
I resemble the color of those she should talk to.

I'm begging you, dear canvas...
It's time to reveal this ugly truth and erase me forever.
I hope you never have to see me again, not ever.

Don't worry, I won't miss the beautiful
clean canvas renewed for eternity.
I pray you're painted with brushes of love,
dressed in ornaments of adornment and
nourished in milk and honey.

Please never allow yourself to be painted by
me again. Make sure that I am forever hidden.

FACE OF BEAUTY
Lyrical the Poetess

Beauty, not just skin deep. It's within you.
The way you carry yourself and treat people too.

The essence of beauty is love and grace.
Not just vanity, self-love, or a pretty face.

Reflection is seen in those you raise.
When they are complimented it procures your praise.

Your children will also reflect and shine.
If the beauty of their mother's intellect is refined.

Prettiness is found in mirrors, vanity in self-admiration.
Beauty is found inside and out, reflects love worth imitation.

With strokes of insight by what you say and do.
Paint the world each day and make it beautiful.

A MOTHER'S LOVE
Lyrical the Poetess

You are a superhero with powers special in many ways.
You care for our family day after day.

Strong enough to deliver life into the world,
yet docile enough to relate to that inner girl.

You have many roles...
You're my doctor, maid, cook, therapist, and a great provider.
A true confidant, your love teaches me to encourage and inspire.

You taught me how to be the best I could be.
By allowing me to express myself and truly be free.

A true warrior who fights to the death
with anyone who tries to bring me harm.
I know the best refuge for me is in your arms.

You are a beautiful Queen with elegance and grace.
No one in the world could ever take your place.

You're a rare gift from God, a true gem like no other.
My mommy, this precious woman, I lovingly call MOTHER.

OUR LEGACY
Lyrical the Poetess

Confidence feels good when enhanced, but sometimes our youth
have self-doubt. It makes them feel like they have no chance.
In my heart of hearts, I know it's their time to shine,
so, I pray they defy the odds and stay on their grind.

Teach them to be true to themselves and honest with others.
View all people as we truly are sisters and brothers.

Teach our legacy on how to respect rules and regulations.
It's for their own good and protection.

Safeguard our society and community because they are our next
generation. These prodigies we birth forth look to us Patriarchs
and Matriarchs for direction in love, self-worth, and education.

It's our God-given responsibility that we don't
mislead our youth into believing everything is the truth.

Stay present in their lives. Don't leave it
up to men of deception and
sugar coaters to blind them with lies of deceit.
Teach them self-awareness and how to use discernment to see
through the unsavory characteristics of the Beast.

Articulate, inspire, and stimulate their minds.
Build up our future intellectuals so they will blossom in full bloom.
Though looked at as the minority,
they will be the elephant in the room.

Knowledge is power when used in wisdom
as we impart it to the new generation.
After all, they are our legacy, our vision, and creation.

GAME OF LIFE
Lyrical the Poetess

Breaking all the rules,
my King's playing Russian Roulette,
thinking this game is cool.

Getting schooled on the street.
Taught how to rob Paul and shoot Pete.
Now you running around scared to meet your defeat.

In jail doing 25 to life in a cell
or Pete's boys sending you straight to hell.
Karma is poetic justice indeed.
If you ain't about that life, King, take heed.

You will reap what you sow.
So, will you plant your pot of weed and a spot,
or will you plant seeds for your family's lot to grow?

The choice is yours.
Money, Drugs, and Power come with a price.
Mourned loved ones, Cages, or your Life...

Sometimes in this game of life,
you lose by the choices that you choose.
Be strategic and think hard, King...
It's your Move!

ENTREPRENEURSHIP
Lyrical the Poetess

Fell off the grid for a while, getting thoughts in order.
Ready to take the world by storm, crossing borders.

Learning a new language, building vocabulary and life.
Helping families plan ahead for when they shut their eyes.

Leaving the next generation with enough funds to handle affairs
and carry on. Nothing left to chance. No stress over money or
possessions when it's time to mourn.

Life is too short and unpredictable; we have to plan ahead.
Not just for death but diseases that many people dread.

Yes, there are living benefits now because
people are stricken with cancer or terminally ill.

Most are not aware of the acceleration of benefits
that cover your care and are just as important as having a will.

Anything I learn, I love to share with those I meet
as I come and go.

Know one. Teach one.
Grab the opportunity to help anyone and their family grow.

I've been searching for financial freedom for a long time.
Tired of grinding for the rich while I nickel and dime.

It's official. I'm a Licensed Agent for Life, Accidental, and Health.
Building my own company as I teach others
and share the wealth.

SIGNS OF THE TIMES
Lyrical the Poetess

Remember the time when we could walk to the corner store?
No worries. Playing tag, hopscotch, hide n go seek...
Games galore.

Boys in the street playing skelly and marbles or messing with
the girls. Knowing they're crushing on us, tryna hide it from the
world.

Mr. Softee, the ice cream truck pulling up around three o'clock.
Kids and their parents come running from everywhere on
the block.

Ah, the block parties. Those were the best!
Neighbors together uniting.
We had love for our street.
Ate and danced all day, partied, no fighting.

We left our battles on the dance floor and still walked away
as friends. Looking forward to the next weekend party,
so we could do it again.

Then the eighties came around, and the new drug Crack
was abound. True love, trust, loyalty and friends were lost like
ghost, could not be found.

Turf wars for the Crack game on 116th, clear down to
Rockaway Boulevard. Seeing people I grew up with
get strung out and killed left me forever scarred.

Shots ringing out on the block became the norm.
Young knuckleheads had guns.
Brothers killing one another for money, respect, or drugs.
No more fist-fights or fair ones.

It's amazing how the Signs of the Times could change life in a
decade. From united households to broken families, divided
and dismayed.

LACK HISTORY
Lyrical the Poetess

Black history month is in our midst.
Our children are murdered like they're on a hit list.
It doesn't matter, February, March, April, or May.
Our children are still dying day after day.

Real Estate Moguls are trying to rule the world.
Men marrying men, girls marrying girls.
No wonder our youth are misdirected and confused.
Exposed to so much hypocrisy and lies as a result of power misused.

In a world with no morals; girl's skirts too high, boy's pants too low.
Our generation labels one another as Niggaz and Hoes.
The future looks grim when no one can be trusted.
Those who supposed to protect and serve are even corrupted.

Where do we go? What can we do?
Is there light at the end of the tunnel? Can we get through?
Yes, if we search for God and His Son; the word, the truth, the life.
Pray for our people. Stop the violence and end the strife.
Lift each other up with love. It's time to unite.
No need for swords or guns, it's a spiritual fight.

See this war is bigger than us. We have no control.
Satan doesn't care what color we are. He wants all of our souls.
Don't worry, he's no match for God. There's a plan in place.
One day we will live forever on earth as one United Race.

BEAUTY AND THE BEAST
Lyrical the Poetess

Beauty is skin deep, nothing is what it seems, so I pretend.
Deep scars are hidden within.
Killing them softly with my devious grin.

Survival of the fittest, what doesn't kill me only makes me stronger
so I pace myself, got you winded. Those who run faster, die younger.

I'm the original Bae Bae kid. I lived more than one life.
I don't die, I multiply. It's just me, myself, and I
fighting the other personalities inside. Momma
always called me Sybil, now I know why.

I'll love you to death then break your heart.
Blow you a kiss then rip you apart.
Feed off your fear and my prowess
as you lay prey for your foulness.

I'm the Last Dragon. Watch me smoke as you choke. Got you hazy.
Spit fire in your grill. Finish him! It's a face-off, you don't faze me.
This beauty is pretty insane. Beast mode Crazy. Unleash
this Queen into the wild, trying to escape my identity
is futile.

Caged emotions, words unspoken
is when my freedom ends.
Fighting the rage as I rip up the stage
with just a pad and a pen.
My Beautiful mind had you blinded by the Beauty,
not the Beast within.

BREAKTHROUGH
Lyrical the Poetess

Am I naive to believe, I can spread my wings? Setting goals
to accomplish my dreams no matter what life brings or am
I a prisoner by design allowing wickedness and evil men
to change my mind?

Feeling pity for myself, my heart is crushed due to reports
of fallen sisters and brothers. Deep sorrows of grief, sitting
here in disbelief. Now that fear has consumed me,
can I break free?

Yes, I will blossom into a beautiful rose in the midst of
weeds and planted seeds of deception. In a world full of
corruption, some liken it to modern-day slavery when we
are killed for voicing our freedom of speech too loud or
expressing our God-given rights not to bow.

I refused to be enslaved by my own penitentiary of mind,
thinking there is no way out. Feeling trapped and
oppressed, I know my Creator loves me, so I'm convinced
I'm blessed.

Even if I face an untimely death as I take my last breath,
doesn't make me a slave or someone not worthy to live
because ignorant men in power went into overkill.

Although it may seem with physical eyes that my life
doesn't matter, the truth is it matters more than it ever
did before.

My redemption was never in the hands of man, it
belonged to the King of Eternity to redeem me,
so even death is temporary.

In a world full of chaotic twists and turns, ups and downs, in a life full of uncertainties, I have an inner peace that can never be taken away. Therefore, the fear of man could never contain me, so I break free from the hype of those who don't believe that salvation lies with God.

No longer a slave in a world of lost hope and misery, not only am I truly blessed but I am truly free.

DON'T LET GO
Lyrical the Poetess

When things are grim and not going well
do I hold on or let go? Only time will tell

A path of destruction is all that's behind me
Do I continue the course or do I set myself free?

There's so much damage, too much pain
How can I fix it, will it sustain?

Will I keep fighting to survive life's blow after blow
or will I succumb to defeat and enter Death's row

So confused, I don't know what to do, I'm lost
Do I take my own life or will I count the cost?

Wait as I calculate, this is an unforgivable sin
Letting go of God's hand means Satan will win

Register in my mind the price of life, now my thoughts
are alright

Depression and Imperfection have loosened my grip
but I choose to hold on tight!

Don't Let Go!!!

EMOTIONS
Lyrical the Poetess

Going through it
Can't get past it
How long will it last?
It comes and goes

Makes me Happy
Makes me Sad
Makes me Cry
Makes me Mad

It's never-ending
Goes Up then Down
Helps me reflect
Feelings Abound

My
Emotions
are
unpredictable

Goes around and around

DON'T
Lyrical the Poetess

Don't say that you care about me, my dear
because if you did, you would be here.

Don't make false promises you know you can't fulfill.
Build up my hope then become a thrill kill.

Don't say you love me if it isn't from your heart.
Actions speak louder than any words your mouth can impart.

Don't come around like a leech only when it's something you need.
I have nothing left to give so take your leave.

Don't come back until you learn how to love yourself.
Then maybe, just maybe you can truly love someone else.

Just Don't...

KNOCKOUT
Lyrical the Poetess

This is my arena. It's time to spar.
Heart to hearts, beat to beats, bar to bars.
Step to me, toe to toe. Give me all you got.
No amateurs here. Rookie, take your best shot.

Knuckle up, son, and guard your grill.
Ms. Thrilla in Manila, coming in for the kill.
Not throwing bows or mighty swords,
I just need one mic and some powerful chords.

Silence your mouthpiece, you're no match for me.
Can't Dodge my flow like Camacho, bob and weave.
My lyrics cause aneurysms, blow for blow.
Landing punches, pound for pound, T.K.O.

Total Knockout, no counting needed.
The Queen Lyrical is still undefeated.
I'm still the Greatest Champ, there's no denying.
Knocked you out cold, but you kept on trying.

YOUR SMILE
Lyrical the Poetess

I feel you watching me from across the room
as our eyes meet, they began to dance.
It enchants me as they employ me to come closer.
Now I'm lost in your trance.
I'm mesmerized and hypnotized by
your eyes, your glance.

It's too late to look away you have me engaged.
Still dazed and amazed,
I smile back cheek to cheek with unspoken words, meek.
The physical attraction is loud and clear, my dear.

Those lips of yours full yet slightly slanted as you grin,
I gaze to see the man within. It's intriguing I must admit
as you can see your reflection in my eyes so brightly lit.

Yes, by the rays of your sunshine emits beauty both in yours and
mine. Shall I approach, take a chance on romance or stand here,
and stare for a while? One thing's for certain... I love your smile.

THE UNHEARD CRY
Lyrical the Poetess

Covid19 in 2020, it's grim with the weepers.
My skin is crawling with fear,
"Jeepers Creepers".

Consumed with heartache as our people are brought to the hospital
to die. A place that was once a refuge to help us fight and survive.

It's crazy how emotions are running wild.
People are going through adverse extremes.
Some panicking, while others are calm and mild.

People can't seem to follow through on a simple command.
Just stay home if they can.

They have theories of their own so they still choose to roam.
Not realizing their actions are causing their family and others harm.

Doctors and Nurses have to play God
and decide who lives and who dies.
They only saved those they thought had a chance,
while the others were literally left in God's hands.

Due to shortages of equipment and resources, we couldn't
hear silent cries from patients with no rights and no voices.
For those still in denial roaming around without a mask,
Stop causing innocent people their demise is all I ask.

I beg my God to fill your heart with love and wisdom
to listen to the unheard cry and please stay inside.

RIP TO ALL THOSE WHO LOST THEIR LIFE TO COVID19

LOST HEARTS
Lyrical the Poetess

Two hearts beat when one is winning, the other will lose
Constant struggle for one heart that's divided and confused

Can't seem to choose between the two,
they're both good in their own way

One gives attention, the other shows no
love but provides day after day

Selfish desires want them both to fulfill a need
Chivalry, romance, lust plus financial security equals greed

This heart is cold and broken, leaves pieces all around
Take casualties of war, fighting for a love that could not be found

Lost the battle because she couldn't choose who goes or who stays
All hearts lose when they succumb to the Queen of Spades

HEARTBEATS
Lyrical the Poetess

It's a new day, a new year. Blessed to still be here.
Time for inspirations, aspirations.
Good intentions, not to mention how proud I am of my two loves.
The best gift from God above.

I set the pattern to work smart, play hard
while I stay on my grind racing against time
to leave a legacy for these two Queens, my heartbeats.

Every move I've made from their birth,
I wanted to instill a Woman's worth
to help them stand firm and learn not to depend
on men who use and abuse, but on
God whose love always remains true.

Love themselves and reflect the love and admiration I have for
them to the next generation. Shine bright like the gems they are.
My prodigies, my stars.

When it's my turn to Rest in Peace, I want them to know the love I
have for them is eternal. It will never cease.
Just look in the mirror, that's where I'll be.
A reflection of you, my two heartbeats.

Smile and shine beautifully for I've given you both the best of me.

Love,
Mommy

IRREPLACEABLE LOVE
Lyrical the Poetess

To my mom, my best friend.
I will love you forever. Our love has no end.

Your love is so deep, your heart so kind.
You're a royal gem, a rare find.

I'm scared right now because I know you're leaving here.
However, your strength and beautiful spirit help conceal my fear.

I know you told me not to be sad and to be strong.
To want you to stay and suffer is selfish and wrong.

Jehovah will comfort me as I mourn and grieve.
Don't worry I'll be in the best hands when you leave.

I thank him each day for the gift of life he gave through you.
A loving mother, shopping partner, and my best friend too.

I just want you to know I'm honored and blessed to have you as
my mother. You are truly irreplaceable like no other!!!!

I love you, Mommy. RIP

Love,
Your Lyrical Poetess~

www.ingramcontent.com/pod-product-compliance
Lightning Source LLC
Chambersburg PA
CBHW040742250626
47164CB00001BA/4